# POETIC MESSAGES

*of*

*Love and Life*

notionpress.com

# POETIC MESSAGES

*of*

*Love and Life*

BARNABAS GUNARAJ

notionpress
.com

**Notion Press**

Old No. 38, New No. 6
McNichols Road, Chetpet
Chennai - 600 031
First Published by Notion Press 2016


ISBN 978-93-5206-706-0

# *Dedication......*

When dreams of success burn inside,
Moulds of a vision does coincide,
To enforce a task towards the goal,
Forges forth body, mind and soul.
Fear not what the future does hold,
Whether failure or bouquets untold,
Only for many a selfless sacrificial deed,
Mortal memories remain immortal indeed!

*Barnabas Gunaraj*

*a tribute in homage to*
Dr. A.P.J. ABDUL KALAM (1931–2015)

# Contents

# Foreword

My friend Barnabas, a budding yet prolific writer nonpareil, has composed a few poems focusing on themes varying from “love,” to “Societal attitudes,” and on “Reverence to the Almighty.” The poems invigorate the senses, kindle a feeling of love and passion in the heart, fill the air with romance - in short, they have an electrifying effect on the body and soul, transporting the reader to a realm of joy, mirth and ecstasy.

He has also penned a few articles (which are a must-read for anyone who relishes humour!) portraying the witty and humorous disposition of the author, and making him an ‘endearing personality’.

Three cheers for ‘LOVE’ and the ‘writer’ (of course!)

Now bask in the warmth of his compositions.

I wish him luck with this book, and his future endeavours...

**a peer and friend**
**(who doesn’t wish to be named)**

# Preface

I do not think I am a poet or writer, and am myself totally surprised at the outcome of the lot of poems and articles herein. I do wish to think that it is all inspired by God's own Word, and are His little messages of life and love, jotted down at the speed of thought. Those written in a spur of a moment give me great joy, although I wish to cherish some others, as those to be God's own dictations to this lowly frame of mine.

Being human I sure was proud, until one day I found that all things that happen at their particular time is not because we do it in that way, but because we are part of a plan, and, God thought it to be done that way. Even now I believe, my book being published, and you reading this - is all part of His wonderful plan. Hope God will touch some part of your heart, through this book so that, I can be happy to have done a portion of my mission given to me!

**Barnabas Gunaraj**

# Acknowledgements

A whole lot of thanks to my wife Hannah ("Georgie") who I always depend on for everything and sundry...right from the foraging out - of my long lost poems (from places unknown) to the typesetting it on a computer....to being by my side to see this in printed form, and more!!

# Messages of Love

# Beauty Within

Everything that
I see you do
makes me only more
appreciative of you.

Each of your movements
graceful and smooth
carries me closer to
beauty and truth.

Submissive and meek
even as you speak,
your pearly smile
lights up the earth.

Beholders of your charm
are far, far too many....
but thanks for showin' me
your beauty within!

One which overflows
to the outside world,
much to the delight,
of the likes of me!

True beauty lies not in
the beholder's eyes,
but inside the person
where the heart resides!

# Everytime

Every time you pass by me,
my heart just skips a beat.
And every time you give a smile,
A chill runs down my spine.

Every time you look my way,
my knees feel weak as straw.
And every time you say a word,
I struggle to cough a reply!

Every time you stand beside,
my body goes stiff as stone.
And every time you say goodbye,
I feel so terribly alone!!

# The Only one . . .

I wanna be the only one
I wanna be the one
I wanna be the one for you
I wanna be so true!

I wanna be the only one
I wanna be the one
I wanna be the only one
if 'ever you wanna have fun!

I wanna be the only one
I wanna be the one
I wanna be the one out there
if 'ever you have to share!

I wanna be the only one
I wanna be the one
I wanna be forever true
caring whenever your blue!

I wanna be the only one
I wanna be the one
I wanna be by your side
if ever your being tried!

I wanna be the only one

*I wanna be the one*
*I wanna see your sunny smiles*
*Though your away by miles!*
*I wanna be the only one*
*I wanna be the one*
*I wanna be forever yours*
*Till breath in me endures!*

13.12.2007

# Nostalgia

Nostalgia is like a disease,
the feeling that envelops
like a cool windy breeze!

I feel like I'd drown
in these memories -
like a King sans a crown!

A royal feeling inside
drives me crazy
as if you are beside!

Oh what turbulence
erupts within me
by thoughts so dense!

Of you my dear
I do reminisce
In bubbles clear!

Not anyone around
Can destroy at all
Nostalgia - so sound!

05.08.2011

# My Crazy Heart

How do I restrain my heart,
Leapin' for joy on seeing you!
' don't get too excited,' I whisper,
'she mayn't have been made for you.'
But my crazy heart -
it doesn't heed me, or my
reprimanding advice.

It just goes running after,
someone far above my price.

How do I make it understand
that the world will not allow,
An entwined soul and a lonesome one,
to mix 'n' mingle, together so!

It's too late to explain right now
that colour plays its role -
No more is he bothered that,
my skin's a trifle - lighter than coal!

But crazily he pines for you,
though your's is akin to snow!

Don't want his enthusiasm shattered,
Or himself fractured into two,
So hesitatingly, I let him be,
In his world of fantasy!

One day his folly he is to realise,
That his dreams are not to be,
But I just can't to the occasion rise,
Breakin' the news to him - you see?

Jus' wondering if you'd care to help,
The next time you pass us by,
Could you please step inside a moment,
or...sound the bell, for us to lament?

# Just a Smile

It doesn't matter
if our love's gone sour,
and you no longer see
what you'd seen before.

What does it hurt you
to flash your pretty smile
and not treating me...
as I were never your friend?

By now it's quite clear
to my unrelenting mind
that you'd rather not face
anyone of my kind.

But for goodness sake,
of you I ask a smile,
only to feel happy
for a little while!

I'd prefer not to ask
if you've though this through
or bothered to see
if my feelings were true.

As of what I'm feeling now,
I need just your smile,
To beat this feeling -
that is so blue!

# Threshold of Vice

Like a beacon afar,
the stars above
subtly light up
Life's forbidden path.

Alleys hitherto
dark and dingy
afraid till now
To enter was I.

Painful memories
I wish to erase
in urgent hope
of unlocking the brace.

Hastily entered
into happiness misread
now to a deadline
I tenderly tread.

Desparate to escape
from life's disdain.
I'm on a threshold
guaranteeing more pain.

Momentary distractions

'round me entwine
a noose made of pleasure
o'ver this neck of mine.

Can't seem to decide
if its' worth its while
but why not indulge
if it makes me smile?

# Endangered Heart

My heart is in danger
when it is in your hands...
I thought you'd
keep it safely
So I'd given it to you...
But ever since you've
met another,
I'm no more
your life's centre!!

Beg you... give back my heart,
I can't bear it any longer,
Don't just throw it away
it couldn't make me
any stronger!
Just leave me alone
think of me as a stranger,
but till you return my heart
keep it safe as in the start.

Had I known you're just a hunter,
more careful I would have been
before handing my heart over
to someone smiting like you.

I'd be a torch bearer
of all lovers in distress...
To satisfy your hunger,
or maybe it is lust...
Don't put my heart in danger
or all lovers would lose -
in Love - their trust!

# Chasing a Dream

How do I stop chasing a dream
A dream as charming and bright
One so filled with bliss and warmth
From one which I cannot stray!

How do you say I should not try
To think and dream all day
When something sweet, as sweet
as this
Gets stuck in memory!

How can I ever end the hope
That you chose to kindle in me
Or forget the times, which skidded by
When your words were my
ardent desire!

How do you call it just a dream
a passing thing to overlook
When each and every breath
I take
Is only for your sake!

How shall I move on like you say
When you are gone away
I dare not dream of those
treacherous days
Spare me some mercy I pray!

How many days do I chase
this dream
You mirthfully filled in me
Or even attempt in futility,
To think
It isn't till eternity!

15.01.2008

# The Snap

An open heart,
with total trust,
a life sustaining part,
into your hands,
I blindly thrust,
With a hope, of
acceptance.

A simple remedy
to soothe the pain,
of a complex malady,
from you to strain
I tried my best
My trials all now vain!

From my heart's deepest
In a tiny time warp,
to quench my thirst
for creative flair,
I needed...a
remnant - of your "snap."

Just the thought of having it,
gave me such a thrill...
but you chose - to belie it
and all my hopes to kill!

# The Façade

Bound by a vow,
extracted by a beau.
Hesitatingly I don -
a happy façade.

Torn to shreds
by hypocritical beings,
my heart just beats
in tempos vain.

For my life, I no more care,
with troubles growing
too much to share!

What is the need,
for this life unnatural,
though I deeply feel...
I will never ask of anyone
'cause answers...
I'll never find!

I would have torn
this mask apart,
and broken promises,
so made to amend,
if it was to a total
stranger...
and not to a trusting
friend!

# Folly

Am I just another
walking down the streets,
yearning for a lost one
beyond my wildest dreams?

Although your smiles,
bewitch me so,
your love to another
isn't hard to see!

I'm not blaming you,
it's my folly I know...
for mistaking your friendship
To be love in full flow!

# Heart in Pain . . .

My heart writhes in unbearable pain,
Watching you wait for hours in vain,
What grave a blunder I blatantly made,
For you did wait, my sight you craved!

What I did not want, this many days
In a moment came out in furious ways
I did not expect for even a moment that
Love so tender, be scourged this flat!

Am I to blame that I am made like this
I wanted to give you, only pure bliss
I hurt so much in my deepest confines
And only for you, my dear heart pines!

I would only do something to help you sew,
Never wanted to see you frown or bow,
To mend your heart and our aching souls
I'd turn the world around on its poles!

What have I done to my darling's smile
And that glance that endears a mile,
Am I so wretched that I did not care,
My only beloved's troubles to share?

My heart writhes in unbearable pain,
My whole being it hangs in shame,
What friend am I if I could not afford
To elicit only the sweet love I adored!

24.11.2007

# Waiting for You

When you are gone
Even for a while
My heart grows heavy
Brooding 'bout your smile.

Longing to hear
the sweetest sound...
of trinklets
'round your ankles fair...
Each step ringing
a note so sweet,
sheer music to my ear.

Against all odds
I hope each day
to see you by my side...
Even though I know
for sure
your future, isn't with me!

Though the roads
that we now tread
may never meet again...
Remember this
my pretty one
you once,
had a friend, as me!

# Pretending

It's no use pretending
that I do not like your smile...
For it's your pearly flashes,
that make my day -
worthwhile.

It's no use pretending
Like I do not think of you
Coz in my mind,
you are embedded true
whether happy,
or feelin' blue.

It's no use pretending
not to need you by my side...
A look at my pillow,
and you would see...
Just how much, I've cried.

It's no use pretending
Like I love you no more...
I loved you before,
and I love you now,
And shall do so,
evermore!!!

# Hurting Me?

I know you'd think I'm crazy,
To carry on loving you,
'spite of bearing the insults,
You've poured by heaps on me.

I care no more for wounds that pain,
Or for the scars they leave,
Because they weren't intended for that,
Is what I genuinely feel.

Were they directed at me to learn,
That your love was not for me,
or was it to escape retribution -
of the shame of giving in.

I truly think and am probably right,
that you do love me still,
and that, those insulting barbs of yours,
Hurt you, much more, than me!

# Like the Way I Feel

An ocean wide would,
have filled up full,
if I'd cried like
the way I feel.

A volcano would,
have fizzled out cold,
if I'd cried like
the way I feel.

No desert would be,
Dry anywhere,
if I'd cried like
the way I feel.

No more would heaven,
need to send us rain,
if I'd cried like
the way I feel.

Never before have
I felt so sad
And now the time
draws near...

Can't imagine how
I'm gonna cope
when to life's
new road, you veer.

# I Just Don't Know

Cold-hearted or sensitive
I just cannot see,
are you affected
by what's happening to me?

Don't you feel happy
or saddened at all,
by all the many events
that the world has in stall?

Are you just ignoring,
my passes at you...
or is there no compassion
for real towards me!

Are you just moody
I ain't able to tell
'coz at times you're friendly
and sometimes not well!

Am I just your buddy
for times that don't pass
as when you're with another
you look through me like glass!

I'm not sure time will heal

the tear in my heart
if you'd say you don't love me
And that it's better we part!

Sure, that, I'd face gladly
bearing the pain till the last
but not that you did love me
but had it hidden in a cast!

# Time's Less Now

Time is so short
I wonder why
I couldn't have
known you then!

There is so much
to talk about......
if only I'd
known you then!

It pains, for now
you love someone
who's dearer than me
I'm sure!

If I'd been
born before my time...
Would it have
been different
had I known you then!

# To Know Your Mind

D'ya care 'bout the way
I'd be,
or just two hoots is what
you
Feel for me?
Wonderin' 'bout those
careless weekdays,
spent by the Boulevard,
the drome, and the plays!

It'd be easier to scale a
mountain,
or swim across
the widest ocean,
than to find what lies
deep,
Inside your mind - that,
With just a peep!

Yet, I dare to ask for
exploring
your exploits - creative!
Taking the liberty
is distinctive -
for me alone I do
presume....
B'coz my thoughts
Forever,
You do, totally consume.

I ask just an insight -
a drop if you prefer -
of your delicious mind,
which,
I surely hope you'd offer.
If all of your poetry,
you aren't naïve to show,
I'll settle for a poem,
li'l of your mind to know!!

# Inspiration

When you are gone,
I just don't know,
How I, will get along!

You inspire me,
to dizzy heights,
As easily as a song!

Fresh dreams for me,
you've made to feel,
can become a reality!

Will I be able to carry on,
What you instill, in me so strong,
Or will the mission just fall apart,
Once you have left, and gone afar?

Fear not that somebody may replace,
the sole position which you now grace,
as no entity as you, be sure,
This our Earth can embrace!

Only memories rare,
that never fade,
remain now to inspire!
Even for a million pounds,
these I'll never trade,
Even long after the...
g'bye's you'd have bade!

# Your Song in Me

Can't get myself to sleep,
Even after a long days' work
Not able to fathom what
Has suddenly gone all wrong.
Tossin' and turnin'
I hear a very pleasant tune;
You've put a song in my heart!

I've never felt this way before.
Butterflies flit crazily in me,
Each time you do pass me by.
Words you utter by my side,
From my heart I cannot hide.
The song it sings forever now,
It won't for a moment subside!

I'm lost in my thoughts...
aplenty rushin' through my head.
If you find me gazing at the stars,
without a care for the world around,
Be sure it's not me in a dizzy
but that song you put in me!

Take me higher - higher,
I just have to say.
Your music does what
None did essay.
What joy I find in that

Little tune of yours,
I will never be able
To clearly explain,
B'coz there are no words to spell
Just music - that makes
My heart, to swell!!

# Love Me?

Do you think of me
As often as I do
And do you smile
The way I smile
When I remember you!

Are you as perplexed
And, as confused as I
When wondering 'bout
Our friendship
That many feel should die!

Do you actually miss me
As much as I miss you
During the long long weekends
That seem like eternity
And does that make
You feel sometimes...
As helpless as I feel!

Do you love me just as much
As much as I love you
Or do you prefer
It not to express
As it's not, what society
will approve?

# A Change of Heart?

After being friends so long
I feared to face another dawn
'fraid someday He would amend
This our friendship to its end.

The tiniest of smiles and fleeting glances
But suddenly supposing that we're poles apart
And this is heading to breakin' of hearts
You try to put it, to an imperious halt.
You suppress your desires
And smother your smiles

Even turn away your discerning eyes.
Stopped kindling the fire,
That once burned within
So we'd wake tomorrow
Without feeling too grim.

Depressing though it seems to be,
And you have sought our pain to free,
Does it matter, in this last hour,
A few more smiles to shower?
I do not ask for deep commitment
Or shatter a seven-step Holy agreement

But only hope you'd never forget
Our paradoxical friendship
Which took its own time to set!

# Search

With utter distaste
I wander here and there
coaxed and cajoled into
a trip beyond compare.

Promised by my kith and kin
To be safe for sure, no doubt
and surely be able and along
to save my sacred skin.

Off we went a maiden searchin'
hoping to dismay the damsel.
For previewed glances so disturbing
And quite as much,
even a trifle disheartening.

Aimlessly we trooped in view,
Though,
surprisingly her heart a' pounded.
I too stood, totally grounded,
when I heard a silent whisper...

Here's the one you always searched for.

# Anything Wrong?

Friends spurn me
Others scoff,
The garden of life
Lies all forlorn.

Love I did crave for
Never will I deny,
But not for me to sleep with
I swear I did not try.

To share my world of sorrow
I wandered here and there,
Nowhere did I find solace
So a buddy's bosom did share.

It is no fault of mine I guess
For the world has been so cruel,
And is it wrong, for me I ask
To hold on to someone I care!

# Innocence

Innocence is what I looked for
innocence is what I sought
that is what I thought I got
not knowing what I was in for!

The first few moments were so fair
in bliss I was too much afloat
when suddenly you began to gloat
and blamed it coolly on evil glare!

It is beyond my comprehension
what great a blunder I had made
for all my happiness I've had to trade
belying hopes of a lovely mission!

Dreams galore of yesterday
lay shattered - how we do not know,
to this world I must bow low
for showing where priorities lay!

No happiness in these worldly lands?
spending your days in pious wait,
shows you the way to Heaven's gate,
Where innocence lies upon its sands!

# Glad You Care

I'm glad you understand
how much I value your smile
and all the little things,
that you so often do!

I'm glad you're sensitive
to how much I need you,
and thoughtful care you take
my life doesn't hurt anymore.

I'm so glad you love me
'spite of many thorny hurdles,
and the way you soothe me
when I come to you in pain!

I'm so glad you care enough
to think about my words
and help me in my essays
to overcome all life's trials.

I'm glad you say you're a friend
at a time when all seems lost,
and also proving you really mean it
standing by me, not feeling shy!

I'm glad you do accept
the humble tripes I gift
though against your wishes it be
These tokens have no price, you see!!

# Special?

Am I just an acquaintance
to you along the way...
or, one of the million
admirers - filling in your day!

More than a few moments
you turn to ones of bliss...
just by your pretty presence
or a smile upon your lips.

I can't understand
why I feel this way
though I be ordinary to you...
You'd, for me be special
forever - come whatever
it be!

# Love so Deep

I'd never reach this depth again
Nor as happy as this, will ever be
I feel a happiness
I'd never attain,
Sure not in this life
That I'll ever feel.

I'd never scale this height again
Nor succeed as now,
When you're beside me!

I'll never feel
so much love again
because I know
None can sweeter be!

# True Friend

So often have been lines or verse
written about true friends
about the bonds of closeness
that pals do always share,
and of the way
they stand side by side
through all
Life's toughest tides.

This is just...
a tiny reminder
to express
how much it means,
to have you as a friend
right now
and hopefully till the end!

# Isn't it Sad?

Isn't it a shame
is it not a pity
that I'm not
the smartest one!

Isn't it so sad
and my dirty luck
that I'm not
as rich as them!

Isn't it disgusting
and so unjustified
that two more shades
have been spread on me!

Isn't is so bad to know
and be often reminded too,
I may not be the one...
Who your dreams enthrall.

# Time Flies

Helplessly I stand and stare
as time just slips away
it feels almost like
the finest sands
that slips
right through my hands.

However hard I try to get
a little hold on time,
it only seems
to move on swifter
like the time
you spent with me.

# Love – for the Bold

Love knows not any barriers
it needs no kith or kin.
Caste or creed it does not see
o'er such matters does trample free!
Cares not for you colour
or 'bout any worldly charm
Whether married or single,
dares disturb your calm!

Love sees no proper reason
or consequences its actions bear,
whether it leads to a heartache
or a wonderful life to share!

Even the timid are smitten
by arrows off Cupid's bow
as often as it shows up
on a bold lover's brow!
Yet,
Love bends for none other,
than the bravest of all hearts
who'd gallantly fight
for their beloved,
and for who
they'd breathe their last!

# Lest my Heart Break

You're tryin' so hard
Not to catch my glance,
Lest I feel love grow
Stronger for you.

You're tryin' to dodge
Coming in my path,
Lest I get deeply
Involved with you.

You're tryin' to hide
Your lovely charms,
Lest I get enchanted
E'en in my dreams.

You're tryin' to stifle
Your pretty smile,
Lest I get carried
To a world afar.

You're tryin' to smother
My love for you,
Lest my heart break
If you aren't for me!!

# Am I so Easy to Forget

Can't get you off my mind,
however hard, or much I try.
Wherever my thoughts
I lead astray
you always come
right in the way.

It's just so crazy
to feel like this,
after you called
our love a mistake.

You ask me how
I think this to be true,
As it has never
Been said by you.

In the manner
you look away,
and the strain
it takes you
to smile each day...
I find it hard to
believe myself
not being in your thoughts,
as you rule my day.

You to forget,
if you do ask
I fear that will be
An impossible task...
I wonder if
you really want
the times we've spent,
to erase from memory

Is it because
of shame in your gut
or am I just,
So easy to forget!

# Twilight of a Friendship

Is it the twilight of our bond?
So many happy moments' already gone
Smote into memory with brisk impatience
Crammed together for lack of time.

Nostalgic moments without compare
We spent together albeit some rare
Cherished forever they will be
Inside this tiny heart in me.

Special though our friendship true
Thoughts afresh, now make me blue
How can we let detractor's obscure
This sublime relation I believe is pure?

A little dust has worn the shine
And made my life truly dry,
Shunned by you
I fear I'd go astray.

Only a few caressing glances
And that pretty ghost - of - a smile,
Make me to live on, to see the morrow,
Never minding, even though I know,
It is bound to present - just more sorrow!

# Good - Bye

Saying goodbye isn't easy at all
'specially to someone like you...
Time has sped so very fast
it's already the hour to part.

Though we know each other well
there's still so much to prove,
I'm just not ready to let go,
until you see me through.

So many mysteries you leave behind
in my tempestuous mind...
so many thoughts yet to be shared
some locked, some tossed 'round.

Good byes forebode a cold finality
that I dread to wish you so...
Let alone now that we part
it's how I feel each day.

We've been through many up's & downs
our lives so much more enriched..
which makes it all so difficult
That hence on, I'll be alone.

I guess it is not possible
To avoid the last goodbye...
but none can ever take away
Your memories, that haunt all day!

# Articles of Life!

# Cricketing Blues

Cricket sells in India. This is surely something that no one in India or for that matter anyone with even a hint of Indian blood, wherever in the world, needs to be reminded of. And it is not a revelation, that I am riding on that very acuity to peddle this article! But, it is not this alone that drives me into penning down some unforgettable (how could one who is hobbling around painfully forget!) moments of glorious simulation of the "Men in Blue!"

I curse not the wise women's intuition (-cum-prophesy?), but I sure hope my wife would have held her peace, as I stumbled out of the house in my new, surprisingly heavy sneakers, and spanking new track suit, which I wore over a blue costume, as a group of my balding friends waited for a "match" which was "fixed" all of a sudden, against the unsuspecting 'youth' of our locality.

How tired we were of playing for the country from our couches! We were determined to show how it is done, considering the years of experience our old gang had trying to educate (from the comfy couch!), our "Blue - Ball Bumbling Bunch" as we called our Cricket Team every time they fanatically grabbed defeat from certain victory! From, (what was a simple taunt [totally uncalled for] from a younger sibling, which touched a raw nerve in the creaking bodies of my zealous team-mates) grew a challenge, between us - "the supposedly over the edge pot-bellied big-mouths" - and, a group of die-hard cricket fans on the lower side of twenty. Recalling the experiences of yester-years, my friends and myself were licking our lips at the delicious lessons we could teach our up-coming lads, in the "art" of cricket as one of my more eloquent acquaintances put it, and unknown to them some nuances of etiquette and 'respect for elders'.

When someone suggested a few weeks practice, there was a concerted pooh-pooh, as we heard about how each of the others had been going for early morning jogs, walks, and, some even to the gym! We were all fit, we declared, even as I hurriedly dismissed a fleeting thought that reminded me of the last occasion I had "walked" - some time before the September rains!

We even slyly included an ex-Ranji player, who surprised us, not only with accepting our invitation, but in addition, nursing one of the biggest tummies in our lineup, which resembled a "Lagaan" team as one of the members in the opposition, tried to put it! We pretended not to hear (how can that be true, when we were all dressed uniformly, and strikingly similar to the real "Men in Blue"!)

Match day was here! Saturday - the perfect day for our exposition, when we shooed away all the other riff-raffs off the nearby playground, into the stands - all too simple with the mighty influence of the local Chairman of our Municipal Council, who (no guesses!) was very much part of our high-profile team! After all it is not everyday that these novices could watch us play and learn from the vast experience we collectively had. Little sacrifices like these would hold them in good stead in their future, was the general consensus, despite the other teams' plea to allow their fellow partners to play in other parts of the ground. No way, we had some hard hitters, and these young critters would have to run all over the ground fetching the ball after all, right? We didn't want our progenies to get hurt running into the other players, while playing on the same ground!

It wasn't a surprise to win the toss either, just considering the noble purpose of our ultimate goal, of being quintessential role models for discipline and, an archetype for the adage "Fortune favours the brave." Our captain couldn't be blamed, but he seemed to have forgotten what to choose, after having called correctly on the toss. A little helpful hint from the other captain seemed to have helped. Whatever transpired heaven knows, but soon we were gleefully on the way, to a batting display, at first instance.

There definitely was a devil in the pitch, or else how could you explain the ball leaving a four-line dotted mark right in the middle of the forehead of our opening (ex-Ranji) batsmen, that too - first ball! He seemed a bit dazed as he was carried off, by six fielders acting like an ambulance - siren and all!

But the exhibition was not going to stop, in spite of the (inexperienced) opposing captain offering to forfeit the match in all humility (?). Though, he did say something which hurt our sentiment, I felt it was only out of certain concern (respect for elders?) that far belied his age. However we would have nothing of that, we were determined to go on like brave warriors, (what is a small aberration in the vast repertoire of ours). In what seemed a century in time, the whole bunch of us scored a half of that in runs, much to the delight of the motley crowd, who we thought were right behind us. It was quite a while later that we were initiated that they were actually "jeers" and not "cheers," but who cares. An uncanny feeling creeped on me that, that the match was quickly over and done with, was secretly welcomed by us all.

We heard there was going to be a 'benefit match' in honour of our convalescing opener, who seemed to have for some reason forgotten that 'once upon a time' he had also participated in some "prestigious tournaments!"

**Barnabas Gunaraj**

# Accomodation Available

It was indeed rather upsetting that we had to leave the comforts of a huge palatial bungalow, in which our 'family' had lived, for over three generations, paying a paltry sum as rent. The surge of high rise apartments swallowed just one more of the spacious "Old Bangalore" style chalet, without remorse - our old owner finally succumbing to the incredible pressure that greed and the land sharks mounted on him!! I do not actually consider him greedy, as he was actually a very nice gentlemen bent over with age, and the whole thing could have been due to those he sired, who want to live life in the fast lane. With their aging father and grandpa sitting on a goldmine in Bangalore, it was not too long before we were packing our incredibly huge amount of 'things' into two lorries.

As we stepped into a rickety two bedroom apartment, that our friend had found us in a jiffy, I could see my wife quickly cover her nose with the end of a pallu, while tightly holding on to our little daughter who was all the while trying to run out of this 'eerie' place. It was not as if the - quite small accommodation resembled some of the scenes out of National Geographic Channel, but there was something looming around, about which I had a strange feeling, I quite cannot express! Suddenly, I spotted a tiny roach, which I squished to a quick exit, before my wife could spot it! Knowing my wife's dislike (to put it very tamely!) for cockroaches, I wished and prayed that It would be the last one that I saw. I was in no mood to further exercise my already overstrained muscles, in shifting to a better accommodation at this point of time!

We had settled down well I thought, when I had started to get good sleep the moment I hit the deck! But it turned out that it was not for long. In fact, I mistook some of the drum beat like noises coming from the kitchen! It was like one of the dreams I got, more like a recurring nightmare, after watching in awe the dark tribes doing an incredibly synchronised war dance, stomping away at the evil spirits I suppose!! Of course, my wife was clothed in much more fabric, as she was chasing a rather swift and nimble cockroach which had teased her all the way into the hall. As I had run hurriedly to check what the commotion was all about, and seeing my wife and the cockroach, doing quite a good job in keeping the timing of a perfect stomp-and-miss samba! I thankfully did not blurt out my thought that I did not know she could dance so well!

Although I had been rudely awoken in my sleep, I thank my stars, that I had the presence of mind, in dismissing another thought - of appreciating her, as the raised broom held in one hand (which I thought resembled the weapon the tribesmen held in their war dance) had actually cleaned up the cobwebs in the rather low ceiling, during the course of her tirade. I could see how livid she was, and I had no time to analyse whether it was at my friend who got us this house, or whether it was only at the cockroach which seemed to mock her, as it sat at a strategic point, just out of reach of both the broom and her stomping 'hawai'.

Just as she was frantically looking out for more apt implements to pry the fellow out she spotted me, and told me (tone, tense etc., changed to protect my image) to join the dance..er.. sorry... to help in exterminating the intruder! I had no intention of telling her right now, that I had spotted a lot many more, during my last sojourn to the kitchen at half past twelve, and that it was not worth the time going after this one lone ranger! Armed with a size 10 chappal, in my right hand, I too was forced to join in the jungle dance, as the cheeky chap raced back into the kitchen! After knocking down some of the vessels and almost hammering the gas cylinder out of shape, I triumphantly produced a dead one! Lucky, I thought to myself, that she did not notice the one she had actually chased, had escaped into a more difficult spot.

That evening, we were off to get something to get rid of this menace, as she too quite did not believe it was the last we saw of these creatures. The cocky salesman, managed to convince my better half that the "Lakshman Rekha" still held its legendary age-old power! She even declined my offer of more effective sprays, which I believed could work better, and over a wide variety of the mini zoo (Only I have seen the lizard chasing the ants, and the spiders enjoying the mosquitos caught in their webs!) Being oblivious to all the other creatures which I have been secretly exterminating, she was in no mood for anything else but the magic lines! I was not sure how long I could keep my hunting game a secret, and I was not inclined to let it out so soon either!

It was only the next morning that I heard her let out of blood curdling scream. Rushing to her aid, I saw a slender ginger-white kitten sneak out of the kitchen window with as much of leftover lollipops as possible in his mouth!! Though I was thankful to this friendly neighbourhood feline for carrying away what I would have had to (grudgingly) have for breakfast, I was quick to console my spouse. I should say I was struggling for words to say, but, it was then that I saw the thick lines (Remember Lakshman Rekha??) around the bowl which held the chicken! Did not have the heart to tell her this was one thing that "no one" expected!!

It was not later that I saw her checking out the columns of "Accommodation Available."

**Barnabas Gunaraj**

# Me! Corrupt?

*(Disclaimer: This article is purely fictional, and none of the person(s) mentioned in this article is/was/are/were personally known to me!)*

It was a hot day, and I was waiting impatiently at one of the apparently defunct traffic lights, in our abundantly blessed city (of traffic and traffic lights that is), when I spotted what appeared to be a blatant case of graft and a pompous display of violation of rules. The case in point was a pot-bellied, be-spectacled traffic inspector, reaching out and accepting a couple of cool(?) drink bottles, which would have become more than warm, as the lot of crates were stacked in an open truck, which zoomed in exactly the opposite way, than what the road sign suggested.

What was equally amazing was the dexterity and speed with which the under-aged cleaner, opened the door of the cabin, whisked two of those bottles from the back of the truck, and passed it on, (with more accuracy than our Olympic relay team's baton exchange), to the Inspector whose arms were both extended to the skies, and then proceeded to settle himself back in the cabin, all in one speedy circus-like articulation, while no attempt was made to even slow down the vehicle, while we all looked on!!

From the dumbfounded looks on the faces of some the beleaguered commuters alongside, I could sense that some witnesses would have cheered aloud like a cheer-leader (with more significance than those displayed by the ones in IPL), watching the antics of an unknown hero! Surprisingly, no one showed any sign of shock or astonishment, at the open display of subornment! Perhaps they were all sympathetic to the Inspector, who after all, bears the heat, not only of the unforgiving Sun (thanks to global warming, brought about by the hideous tree chopping - by the greased hands of another official), but also that of the crowd, itching at the red signal, honking or showering expletives, and that... only when the Inspector was looking the other way! Maybe he deserved a cool drink anyway, but as I surmised why the system could not reprimand him for his misdemeanor, a guy without a helmet fools us all, as he jumps the "red" signal and goes on his way, surely to reach his destination ahead of all of us, who were bewildered and dithering whether to cheer or rant!

While rehearsing to myself, the curious turn of events at the junction, I wondered what exactly has permeated into our "advanced" society, as we no longer seem to have the chivalry, shame or character, to stop what we know is wrong! We all have reasons, and cry to be victims of circumstances, as the very same raison d'être of "severe traffic jam" is muttered to our bosses, even when we constantly reach late to our offices everyday, without a care to think, if robbing the time of our chief employers, is not to be construed as "corruption"! It does not stop at that since we can all discern, when the know-all's in the office arrive, (albeit late!) they do so with such a flourish and perfectly orchestrated mannerism, of having to complete the most urgent project or presentation on their systems, only to be found browsing the net, for personal work, a far cry from the purpose the Internet connection was actually positioned for them! This can't be portrayed as corruption, could it?

Even as the ever growing crowd at the signal, unitedly grew impatient, I couldn't but help notice, all others around me observe, another blatant display of affection, (not that any of the above instances can be read to be such!) yet right amongst the forgiving society, were a couple (newly married or unmarried...who knows or cares), who were oblivious of the ambience, developing around the crossroads, more precisely that of a drive-in theatre, displaying what is a "normal motion picture" nowadays! Going by the living standards of today, and by the behaviour of the couple, it was highly unlikely that any legally married husband, would have the inkling to display such fondness to his spouse to such an extent, that too in such an atmosphere...here again I was led to speculate, if this should also be brought under the purview of "corruption"!

A myriad issues were juggling in my mind, as to how all this will stop, or, at least change for a better and cultured society, and how I would bring all these "crooked" people to book, when I was reminded of, the saying, "Brother, before you remove the speck of dust in your neighbour's eye, remove the log of wood in your own!." Then, again I wondered, who is to judge, or, define what is corruption, and where do we draw the line, or how do we mete out punishment to the other - when all are crammed into a besmirched world, likened to one of a pussy cat drinking milk?

While I myself could not re-collect any instance of any wrong-doing in my life, hard as I tried, and with all my might, I unexpectedly saw the same burly Inspector remove the keys from my bike, motioning me to push it to the side of the road....

The lights had turned green, but this time, not for me, I guess!

# Monkey Trouble

Being usually staid, considerate and least critical about the physical features of anyone I know, I remember never to have even slightly referred to anybody's looks to that of our primal ancestors. A particular channel specializing in bridging the gap between us and our forefathers(?) made me wonder for a little while as to how far we have actually come. I was intrigued by a chimpanzee in Florida, which had actually recognised numbers upto a 100, and managed to play out a song from a song sheet. Something told me this was going to be tough to get over - wondered why!

John and I were on our way to a naming ceremony of a baby born to one of our friends. Once there we waded through a huge crowd which waited to gather around the stunned, yet cute looking infant. He turned his head this way and that, each time a compliment was bellowed into his tiny cradle, from different directions. I wondered from his expression whether he was looking for a familiar doctor to complain about a headache or a pain-in-the-neck! As if my thoughts were relayed by telepathy to John, he quietly whispered to me, asking me what I thought the baby was thinking....... "Maybe monkeys" I remembered to have replied, when the child's grandfather aping a model of a toothpaste advertisement, invited us to have an aromatic spicy lunch, specially prepared by cooks from their homeland.

I was thinking what had got into me, as this "monkey" thing was suddenly caught in my mind, and more forcefully than ever I remembered some idiom of getting rid of this monkey off - the back of my mind. The more I tried it, the more difficult it seemed! Suddenly, one of the boys "monkeying about" (oh, no!), about by the street, darted across. Jamming the brakes and swerving the car to one side I managed to avoid hitting the boy. "Hey you, illiterate baboon!" shouted my pal John. He then turned to me, and asked why I was laughing like a chimp, when I could have easily gone to jail, and that he would only have been able to see me like some gorilla in a zoo. I could not tell him I was wondering about the 'monkeys' in our brain!

Afraid that I would perhaps crash into something else, as I seemed to be in a sort of stupor aided by the heavy lunch, my friend unwittingly went into a conversation about how much stress the little baby would be going through. He most philosophically said, that with so many good meaning relatives, peering down at him as if some new species of - you-know-what had come into being, he agreed I may be right that the baby could well have been thinking, an incessant group of monkeys, were indeed grinning down at him. I am not too comfortable myself with references to our supposed ancestors, despite the progress we have made, nor with the progress the chimpanzee in Florida has made by recognising figures upto 100 and humming my favourite song. Especially since an excruciating and unforgettable experience with Ria my cousin's daughter.

Thinking of Ria I quickly had a change of plan, and though I was to drop my pal, I requested him to accompany me to my cousin's house, whom I had not visited in a long time. I myself in reality forced myself to make this courtesy call, which was long overdue. He joined me, even as I silently rued the last experience I had had, with my cousin's rather outspoken 4 year old. When we had finished the pleasantries, in came Ria shouting her hi's and hello's. Thankfully, this time Ria recognised me to be human, and told my name correctly. John was not too interested in the goings-on as he was busy looking at the delicate artifacts my cousin had collected years. Ria then suddenly turned her unabashed attention to John, who was just then picking up a coconut shell carved into a shape of a chimpanzee, and promptly, pronounced, "Who's this monkey?" I wished John had not heard, while I could see my cousin's face suddenly resemble that of a red-faced baboon. I had always appreciated John's patience, and hoped he would show another ample dose of the same, when he inevitably asked, what Ria had said. My cousin was so flustered that in trying to quickly cough up something, to pacify both John and Ria she actually mumbled... "Er, er.. nothing I think she said, er.., M..., Mu... Muncle, no ma, Ria?" Before she could muffle her daughter's next words, she had already blurted out, "No, I said Monkey."

That was the last time I dropped John to his home and have no idea about his whereabouts ever since.

**Barnabas Gunaraj**

# My Fair Lady!

You couldn't actually call me a spoilsport when I usually undo my wife's efforts to "make up." Not the usual cozying up to me, after a now almost, every day snap and return snap argument, which we seem to surprisingly miss, even if one day passed without one! I am talking about her botched up make up ritual which she goes through everyday, - botched partly due to her strong determination to go through with at least a minimum of make up - when she tries to make do with somewhat heavy doses of powder - and partly due to my rather strong comments (which take a hue of voodoo, depending on the occasion) on the ill-effect of using any "Fairness" cream. Dissuading her from believing such tall claims is so unbelievably difficult, as I needed to actually use all of my persuasion skills which I picked up in the umpteen number of sales training sessions, but with an objective of inducing exactly the opposite response than that of a "Sales Close."

In fact, I don't restrict myself to my spouse alone, and even chide my elder sisters to resist from using any sort of dyes on their hair, especially after someone made an awfully rude remark, calling me their elder brother thanks to my slightly receding hairline. Of course that was not the only reason for my showing dissent to their using dyes, eye-brow liners, fairness creams (bah!) etc., etc., as I actually know that the chemicals in those stuff are just not suitable for the skin. We so often read about the ill effects or non-effects of such creams, in the very same magazines which feature advertisements promising to make even those with the heaviest doses of melanin into air-hostesses! It is such an obsession nowadays, that I take every rare opportunity to expose these conmen, to any woman whom I can safely discuss this rather sensitive topic (wonder why they are all so synchronistical in being touchy when I start to mention anything in this regard!!).

The more I gently oppose this movement, the more I seem to feel resistance, and the most recent being one from my 16 and a half year niece, who's just into college!! Someone who I had memories of being the sweetest and gentlest of my nieces, suddenly came back more vehemently than my spouse, that even my hardened resolve was dented for a moment, and was left stuttering for words, as she walked off raising her well shaped eyebrows and flashing her eyes lined with mascara and shadow!! I could definitely see a smirk on my wife's face although she did try her best to hide it. She could have done that more easily if she had painted her face the way some other women do, almost making their faces similar to a kind of plastic - thus I thought to myself, gathering some positives from this little untoward incident.

Quickly wanting to refurbish my almost waning stand, especially since being painfully isolated with not many a taker for my arguments, I offered to take my better half out for a shopping spree, to one of the many shopping malls sprouting in the city at an amazingly rapid rate. I could not term it a softening of my stand, but when I saw my wife quietly looking at the totally changed façade of today's population of Bangalore, a thought that maybe she felt out of place came to my mind. Would she be able to graduate to such a degree of artificiality, I carelessly wondered aloud, when I felt a piercing pinch in my bulging tummy, from her hitherto unnoticed neatly manicured nails. However prudent and sensible my analysis, I realized it was not worth expounding outside of the "four walls," where I had so far, had that liberty, thanks to her "other side"!

Still reeling from the ambush, we ambled into a huge super market, even as I pictured the thumb drive I wanted to buy, dissolving into thin air. Not one who likes to window shop, I knew my wife was going to pick up just enough of the most "wanted" things, things that I could not veto, but only set back my choice purchase by a few months. As she went scouring for what she wanted at a furious pace, I too had to fill my basket with a few things, at least to avoid the glares of the security person, who I felt was watching me too closely, until I stacked my basket with a few important things! Finally, with both baskets in her hands full (thankfully), she signaled me to stand in the queue while she picked up the last few goodies. My hand itself was itching to feel the rate of my heart beat, but desisted when I spotted two other men in the queue, who already had their hands in their chest pockets.

We came back home, me exhausted in more ways than one, and she with a smile, which I remember to be sported usually by one who had some sort of accomplishment. Secretly I watched her unpack the bags, as I knew she would be surprised at what I had picked up for her, but surely I wasn't ready for was in store. For as she saw the make up kit and fairness creams I had bought for her, she promptly said, "Who told you to get this 'Fairness Cream for Men!!'... just go and return it now, please!." I thought that if I bought her the cream and compact, she would let me try this "wonder" cream. She would have nothing of that!! Guess she's taking my views more seriously now!!

**Barnabas Gunaraj**

# Superfluous Philosophy

This morning I was feeling particularly lazier than usual, and my wife had to hand over my breakfast to me while I was on the sofa reading the newspapers. Seeing the dish I restrained myself from uttering my comments on the preparation, which would make the day nastier than the "nashtha" itself.

As I was reading about a malnourished lot of the Dark Continent, I managed to push a few spoons into my mouth. Suddenly, I realized I could be better off with a bit of sugar, which I was not to touch according to my wife's favourite doctor! (at least not while she was around, I had thought). The question of asking her to bring the sugar bowl from the kitchen to the place where I was...? No need to even think of it! Well, as I mentioned earlier, my physical senses did not permit me to take the walk to the kitchen, nor was I so inclined to be able to think of an excuse to rattle off to my wife, about the reason for my tryst in the kitchen, for, in case I made a noise there, and by chance, if she hears me... I'd have to hear yet another lecture which our doc had already handed me! (And intriguingly, more likely than not, it always does happen... Wonder why the lid crashes to the floor every time "I" open it!) Traversing between thoughts of my inability to take any more of this insipid "uppit," and, risking a few spoons of sugar to make my task simpler, I was almost five spoons into my dish by then!! (Quite an achievement I mused.)

My toddler came close enough, for me to try and coax her to eat one spoon at least. "Phtoo," out it came like a rocket now giving me another unwanted chore, just at a time when I was not in any mood to accomplish anything, and that too a clean-up job to be done without raising a suspicion in my wife's mind (Difficult to say the least!).

For some strange reason I thought of V.S. Rao, a great friend of mine with a supposedly philosophical bent of mind... (another pal calls it thoughtless argumentativeness). I wondered what his observation would have been to this little morning conflict of mine! However, my mind trickled off into superfluous philosophy (like his!), and started wondering whether the world itself may not be working on similar lines!

Remember, how often we stress to others that there is no substitute for hard work, and, we reap what we sow? Well, ever wondered why the person who works smartly from 9 to 9 instead of the usual 10 to 5 like me, earns more? I casually thought of it - what if I were a 12 hour worker? I would have had the urge to spring out of the sofa, rush to the sugar bowl and had a better breakfast, or, rather made it a bit sweeter than it was! (Or better still I would have been on the dining table, a room closer to the sugar bowl!)

Taking the analogy further, I imagined how the medical problem would not have appeared in the event of my general demeanour not being so hopelessly lethargic! Just as a hard working professional is more successful and would probably earn more, thus I could have had a sweeter breakfast! As I was thinking, maybe I could have been....! My extravagant bubble of a dream was suddenly shattered by my better half, "It's 8:30! I told you I got to reach office by 9:00... and... and... what are you still doing with your BREAKFAST???"

My hitherto lazy bones sprang into involuntary action, startling the wits out of my kid, and, surprising me also to an extent! Some thought of "adrenaline" came to me, but no... not now... no time for any more superfluous philosophy... my day had really begun...!

Finished breakfast, and all...

**Barnabas Gunaraj**

# Milky Travails

Straining to get up from the bed early morning, not due to any laziness, but for a strange viral flu, which has rendered me almost totally immobile, I crane my neck to have a peep outside my window, to check out the reason for blaring horns, which seemed more than unusual for the usual traffic jam which piles up at a later hour than this. To my surprise I see the pot-holed ridden road opposite my flat to be partly flooded with the overnight rain, and a driving-school car with a big "L" trying to contemplate how big or deep the ominous looking pothole, just below her left wheel was. This deliberation on the part of the driver had already lined up and long line of vans and autos, ferrying school children with worried little faces.

With the little jam cleared in while with the frantic waving of hands by good Samaritans passing by, it took a while before I took painful baby steps, braving a steady drizzle which had started by now, towards the milk vendor's shoppee. The shrill reminder (of the Doc) from my better half to keep the stiffened legs on the move, helped in hastening my venture to shop.

Trying to be as brisk as possible, I hobbled over the unevenly laid cobblestones, or maybe which had originally been evenly laid, but now undone like a monster's uneven teeth, which seemed to be laughing at my plight. I reach the point where I used to rapidly cross over to the pavement shop, which was just exactly opposite to where I was standing. Little did I imagine or realize what I was going to go through to achieve the little errand that I had set out on.

Just as I stepped on to the road, a seemingly innocuously innocent looking schoolboy on a cycle, whom I assumed to be at safe distance, zoomed past me in a flash, and an antenna like thing from his huge backpack scraping my nose. Hurriedly stepping back on to the pavement, I unwittingly stomped on the toes of a pretty young college damsel, who let out a shriek which brought more eyes on my stumbling form. All my profuse apologizing made no change in her menacing face, as she clutched her little toes, which had turned red as a result of my evasive action! How was I to know that a small army of people, had gathered behind me and wanted to join with me in crossing to the other side. With all the confusion, and traffic halting to see if I was misbehaving or not, the group crossed over leaving me at the same spot, while even the aggrieved college girl, hopped away to the other side.

Terribly embarrassed to the core, I waited a bit for a change of people from the scene before I started embarking on the increasingly tougher job, which had seemed so simple just a couple of months ago. I wondered how my little street had changed in such short time, when I was rendered to the confines of my bed. It seems like a long time since I had gone to fetch milk for the morning cuppa. My waiting for a change of scenario, didn't seem to work as the frenzied crowd looked to have tripled all of a sudden, what with the parents dropping their children, on the way to work, joining the troop of school and college students, on scooters and in their luxury cars.

My task was hardly completed, yet my mind turned to a movie called "Mission Impossible," though this apparently minute job I had on hand, could hardly be termed as a mission, and more so as impossible. Yet as time went by, it did seem so. It was getting ridiculously late for me to get over with this, and was sure my wife would be worried, as to what was taking me this much of time, to get a hold of a litre of milk! Sure enough I could feel the buzzer of my mobile, just as I thought there was a let-up in the traffic after a long time, and it was futile to guess who it would be. I had not enough time to pick up as I had started to dart across the less crowded road, or so I thought, when the blare of a horn piercing my ear, and a mouthful of road rage from a skidding motorist, brought the actual reality to my conscious thought. The words I heard were enough to make my head go into a tailspin, as if the toll of crossing the road in the manner I did, was not enough.

Gathering my senses, while thanking my stars for the "near-hospitalisation" experience, I confirmed it was none other than who I thought it was on the phone. There were three warnings already. Quickly shuffling along to the milk shop, I went with the bag half-open, not wanting to waste any more time. I was greeted by the milk vendor with a queer smile, the sight of which did not encourage me one bit. He said almost chidingly, that he had watched my whole travail, and was signaling to me, not to cross the road, while I was determined to make it to this side! I was miserably filled with angst within, though I tried my best not to make it show on my face. I couldn't care much about it though, with his mirth more than showing on his face. Inasmuch as I was worried about getting back to the other side of the road, the fact of reaching home empty handed was nerve-tingling.

That the world had not a word of comforting was just another lonely thought flitting by. Chivalry I realized was a long lost word in this glitzy modern world whizzing by. I wonder if the word had lost its presence due to us parents not practicing it, by first being models to our children, and yet expecting it from all others in society. Having been caught in the whirlwind of change, I seem to doubt if chivalry is the right word here, and whether it is apt to expect it to be applied to a gentleman in an old man's shoes, due to a debilitating disease, wrought by a mere mosquito, which sometimes even baffles many a learned doctor! Try as I can, I can't fathom the reason why the young ones of today don't realize that the phase I am in could happen to them in a few years, what with time seeming to fly faster and faster, by the moment!

My head was spinning...I came back dazed, with my bag in hand to meet my usually sweet wife, in a mood which switched ends on the sight of the bag in my hand being empty. The tirade of words not registering fully in my head, I was thinking of an ad where a guy brings milk and bowls an imaginary bouncer, with the milk packet, on his wife's head! But...now it was my turn to duck!

**Barnabas Gunaraj**

# MESSAGES OF LIFE

# Psalm 23

Lord Jesus
My Shepherd,
My Provider,
My Comforter,
and My awesome Guide.
Lord Jesus
My Protector,
My Anointer,
My Redeemer,
and Joy fore'r to reside.

**15.12.2006**

# O Holy Spirit..

*O Holy Spirit,*
*Come thou upon me,*
*O Holy Spirit,*
*Make me thine!*
*O Holy Spirit,*
*Now shine upon me,*
*O Holy Spirit,*
*My guiding light!*
*O Holy Spirit,*
*Fill my whole being,*
*O Holy Spirit,*
*With thy love divine!*

10.04.2007

# Teach Me, O' Lord!

*TEACH ME O' LORD, TO EVER BE HUMBLE,*
*LET MY PRIDE, NEVER TO SWELL!*
*TEACH ME O' LORD, TO BE HELPFUL,*
*LET MY HEART, NO CHARITY DISPEL!*

*TEACH ME O' LORD, TO BE YOUR CHILD,*
*LET ME NEVER BECOME UNFAITHFUL!*
*TEACH ME O' LORD, TO KEEP A WATCH*
*LET ME KNOW YOU, KEEP ME STILL!*

*TEACH ME O' LORD, TO SEE THE LIGHT,*
*AND IN OTHERS BRIGHTNESS INSTIL!*
*TEACH ME O' LORD, TO SHOW YOUR LOVE,*
*TO WHOEVER IS ON DEATH'S ANVIL!*

*TEACH ME O' LORD, YOUR MESSAGE TO GIVE,*
*TO THIS WORLD,THAT'S SWATHED IN PERIL!*
*TEACH ME O' LORD, TO SEEK YOUR PEACE,*
*LET YOUR DOMAIN REMAIN TRANQUIL!*

*TEACH ME O' LORD, REDEMPTION TO ACCEPT,*
*AND FOR YOUR KINGDOM, TO WAIT UNTIL!*
*TEACH ME O' LORD, TO PATIENTLY AWAIT,*
*HEAVEN'S GLORIOUS JOY AND THRILL!*

**10.12.06**

# Lord, When...

I wander,
You seek!

I stray,
You instruct!

I thirst,
You quench!

I hunger,
You feed!

I rot,
You heal!

I fear,
You comfort!

I fail,
You console!

I praise
You bless!

I sin,
You forgive!

I repent
You redeem!

26.12.06

# Without You, O' Lord!

WITHOUT YOU, O' LORD, I AM EMPTY,
WITHOUT YOU, O' LORD, ALL ALONE,
I NEED, YOUR SPIRIT, TO FILL ME,
'O LORD, I NEED YOU - TO BE NEAR!

WITHOUT YOU O' LORD, I AM NOTHING,
WITHOUT YOU O' LORD, LIVE IN FEAR,
I LIFT, YOUR NAME, TO THE HEAVENS
MY LIPS DO ALWAY, SING YOUR PRAISE!

WITHOUT YOU O' LORD, I AM HOLLOW,
WITHOUT YOU O'LORD, A DISGRACE,
I NEED, YOUR SOOTHING PRESENCE
IN THIS, UNTIDY HEART OF MINE!

WITHOUT YOU O' LORD, AM NOT WORTHY
WITHOUT YOU O'LORD, FAIL TO SHINE,
I NEED YOUR WORD TO CLEANSE ME,
AND MY SAVIOUR - TO DWELL WITHIN!

WITHOUT YOU O' LORD I AM WAYWARD
WITHOUT YOU O' LORD, STEEPED IN SIN!
I NEED YOUR GRACE TO GUIDE ME,
AND WASH ME, O' LORD, TILL ANEW!

23.12.06

# Mother

*For to this mortal world, I grieve*
*And a bitter loss I share*
*Could not have I been better blessed*
*Without such a sad loss to bear?*

*The one I love, and someone who loved*
*Today I stand without!*
*(Forever, I'll love you Mom,*
*I know you did throughout!)*

*So says the whole wide world to me*
*That with untold regret I am,*
*And that, with pain to brim so filled*
*is reason life feels - a sham!*

*It is quite right and fairly true*
*That I weep inside in woe*
*Yet my soul's trifle happy now*
*For she's reached the other shore!*

*And on this Earth I carry on*
*The mission that He's giv'n*
*With little worry about Mother or me*
*As I wait to meet her in heav'n!*

02.02.2006

# Father to Son

My son, you ask me to return,
the ten grand gift you gave!
Four score grand, you now earn,
A 'mount, I could never save!

You say I am a stumbling block,
to the happy times you crave,
and wish that you were never born,
to parents such as us - "insane"?

Though I'd never expect from you,
to tally up all that we spent,
would be gross and so unfair too,
asking you monetarily to relent!

Can only smile, more in concern,
as I think of Mom's labour pain,
which would easier now be borne,
Than hear those stinging words again!

Will the times of happiness unborn,
wee hours in sacrifice for your sake,
Be priced and in your portfolio adorn,
A parent's love - costed as stake!

Never ever crossed my mind, my Son,
Or even a moment did we ever take,
In pondering the cost of labour done,
Of what it took us, 'a man' to make!

02.01.2014

# Daughter

If you have a daughter or two
remember you have riches untold
though a few sons may be otherwise
If so, you may have already been sold...

When troubles they come calling someday
This world may judge you by your Gold
But the saving grace 'twill always prove
to be daughters who're brave 'n' bold....

From the lost times that seem a blur
Thoughts in a cloud frighteningly cold
Obscure your vision, and even seem blind
Still her smile will be worth the World!

Into the twilight, souls travel alone
With only favourite memories to unfold
As every moment tenderly fleets by
'Tis a daughter's grasp you will behold...

18.11.2014

# A Child

tender feet
the softest bones
and a tiny
oversized head!
It is what makes
the tiniest of forms
within a mother's womb!
Oblivious it lies
of the world outside
probing what it's
going to be!
As even before the
very first cry
does begin
it's battle for life!
For if it turns
into a girl
She could be
Sentenced to die!
O woman!
How can you abet
killing a part of you!
Or rather
how can you forget
it could have easily,
been you!

# Flying High

*BE PROUD, IT IS NOT VICE,*
*YOU ACHIEVE THE FRUITS*
*OF YOUR LABOUR!*

*SUCCESS, BUT COMES, TO*
*A SELECT FEW, WHO DARE*
*WITHOUT SLUMBER!*

*NOW FROM ATOP THE PEAK,*
*BOLD CHALLENGES, NEVER*
*SEEMED SO BLEAKER!*

*YOU SURVEY WITH A SMILE,*
*TORTUOUS TERRAINS, THAT*
*ONCE, WAS TO CONQUER!*

*YET, LET NOT YOUR SMILE,*
*TURN TO A SMIRK, AS YOU*
*GO EVEN HIGHER!*

*FOR SOME DAY, NOT FAR AWAY,*
*YOU MAY SOON RETURN, BACK*
*TO - TERRA FIRMA!*

12.12.06

# Wondrous Works...

Why among this vast expanse
this beast you did create?
Amidst these wondrous works of yours
my species, number great?

When all that's yours, in this wide world,
bow down in reverence,
no sign of gratefulness display,
instead flaunt pride immense!

Infinite beauty you have bestowed,
on a bloom that lasts a day,
but why this wretched one sustain
over four score years - can't say!

Tiny creations hardly seen 'round
blend well into your plan,
yet this blinded spirit of mine,
rejects the "Son of Man"!

Precious the gift of ultimate love
On the cross did demonstrate!
While though no sins of mine remain,
Faithless thoughts do not abate!

Lord, your wondrous works abound,
on which, in awe I marvel!
Save for understanding Your Will,
I pray, do make me humble!

**29.12.06**

# Delight!

BROTHERS & SISTERS IN OUR LORD, DELIGHT!
ON OUR LOWLY SELVES HE HAS SET SIGHT!

IN HIS GREAT MIGHTY WORKS ALWAYS, DELIGHT!
WHEN OUR WAYS WE GO, HE SETS OUR PATHS RIGHT!

IN HIS WORD WE OUGHT, TO EACH DAY, DELIGHT

HIS INSTRUCTIONS TO YOU NEVER SHOULD YOU SLIGHT!

THAT HE IS SO AWESOME, REMEMBER IN DELIGHT!
HE IS THE ONE WHO CAN, SET YOU FREE FROM FRIGHT!

IN ALL REVERENCE, IN HIS HOLINESS DELIGHT!
IT IS THE ONLY WAY, FOR A FUTURE THAT'S BRIGHT!

THAT HE HAS CHOSEN TO SAVE US, DELIGHT!
FEAR NOT, BE BRAVE, UPHOLD THE LORD OF LIGHT!

REDEEMED US FROM SIN, SO IN OUR LORD, DELIGHT!
TO BE HIS ANGELS, IN HEAVEN, LIVE LIFE UPRIGHT!

IN THE KING WHO RULES THE HEAVENS, DELIGHT!
TO GAIN ETERNAL LIFE, INTO YOUR HEART, HIM INVITE!

05.01.07

# Shun not O Lord,

*Shun not O Lord this sinful heart of mine*
*Merciful to extreme is the heart of thine*

*Forgive O Lord this haughty spirit in me*
*Make me as humble as You taught us to be*

*Show me O Lord the righteous path to follow*
*Ready may I be for your return now or 'morrow*

*Help me O Lord my neighbour not to judge*
*Let me no fellow being ever slander or sledge*

*Hide me O Lord from the vile one, I pray*
*Let me not away from your sight to stray*

*Rebuke not O Lord if at times I don't obey*
*Remind me gentle Spirit beside you to stay*

*Spew not O Lord when my faith is lukewarm*
*To your will I surrender my heart to make calm*

**11.01.07**

# Tarried too Long!

SORRY MY SAVIOUR THAT I TARRIED SO LONG,
TO ACCEPT YOUR GOODNESS AND MERCY UNTOLD!
HOW FOOLISH I'VE BEEN INSPITE OF MY SONG,
NOT TO BE FAITHFUL, OR YOUR PRECEPTS BEHOLD!

FORGIVE ME O' LORD FOR SO CALLOUS A MANNER,
AND REBUKE ME NOT FOR BEING SO BLIND!
PRAISE YOU A MILLION FOR MAKING ME SANER;
FOR SHOWING THE WAY TO BE PATIENT AND KIND!

IN ACRES OF LAND AND GOLD I HAD TRUST,
NOT BELIEVING THAT AM MYSELF, ALSO YOUR GIFT!
NOW WHEN IT LAY BARREN AND LADEN WITH RUST;
BELATEDLY REALISE WHERE MY SIGHT IS TO SHIFT!

BLESSED - THE DAY YOU SAVED MY WICKED SOUL,
SAFE IN YOUR ARMS I KNOW 'TWILL FORE'ER BE!
NO WORDS CONTAIN, THE JOY THAT ME MAKES WHOLE,
NOR EXTOL IN FULL, THE SALVATION THAT'S FREE

24.01.07

# Accepted?

O Lord have I been accepted by you?
Have I been enclosed-secure in your fold?
Are angels in Heaven dancing in delight?
Am I as a lost sheep -
precious in your sight?

O Lord have I been sought out by you?
Am I a lost coin among those you own?
Lord have I been really welcomed back?
Am I a forgiven son-
'spite of goodness I lack?

O Lord, has your mercy been poured?
Am I among, those for whom, you died?
Have I been washed as you rose again?
Am I now, a free soul -
On it's way to Heaven?

**25.01.07**

# No Question

Who am I to question, Lord,
whether love's dead or alive?
Being just a worthless thing
how can I not believe?

In mighty grace, you did descend
ignoring our faithlessness,
yet the devil deceivingly fills
unholy doubts in us.
Forgive, my, unknowing heart,
which even your kingship quests,
instead of gracious acceptance,
haughtily rejects your "rest."

Should earlier have been
that my soul be burned
and untold torment to see,
but in your kind, gentle love
you chose to set me free.

I dare not question, Lord
having proved over all doubt
that 'tis you who loved,
first and more,
than this ungrateful lout.

Who am I to question Lord
your mission on this Earth?
For out of love beyond all reason
saved us from a burning "Hearth"!

2.2.2007

# There Hangs My Shame...

There hangs my shame
There hangs my sorrow
My guilt is crucified
On the Cross that's stained!
With His precious blood!

His blood has cleansed me
His blood has purified
My heart once accursed
He has truly now redeemed!
From the Gate of Hades!

Into the depths of Hell
Into the place of death
He went within instead of me
My ransom full to pay!
My captive soul set free!

Jesus My only Lord
Jesus My only King
He conquered death for me
My soul He has revived!
Now His praise I sing!

For Heaven I do rejoice
For Heaven I do delight
As I'd see my Saviour God
And Our Lord Jesus Christ!
On whom rests my sight!

12.02.07

# A Mosquito?

*MOSQUITOS – THEY TROUBLE ME*
*BUZZ IN MY EAR, IN MOCKERY!*
*THEY CARE A LITTLE, THAT I AM BIG*
*UNDER MY NOSE – PERFORM A JIG!!*
*THOSE TINY 'SECTS, DON'T REALISE*
*FOR ME 'TIS EASY, TO PENALISE!*
*UNMINDFUL OF, MY WRATH AND HAND*
*TO DRINK MY BLOOD – ON ME DO LAND!!*
*WITH DISRESPECT, AND UTTER SCORN*
*JAB AND PRICK, MUCH LIKE A THORN!*
*I SHRIEK IN PAIN – AS MY FOE I SLAP*
*IN IT'S DEATH, I GLOAT, I CLAP!!*

*O MASTER YOU, YOUR SON HAD SENT*
*BUT LORD I WAS, SO INDIFFERENT!*
*UNMINDFUL OF, YOUR GRACIOUSNESS*
*MOCKED AND JEERED, PURE RIGHTEOUSNESS!!*
*DID NOT CARE – THAT AWESOME YOU ARE*
*WITH MY SINS, IN DANGER DID DARE!*
*NOT UNLIKE, A PARASITE – I DRANK*
*YOUR BLOOD I SPILT, IN YOU, THORNS I SANK!!*
*IF YOU CHOSE, I COULD HAVE DIED*
*BUT AT MY PRIDE, YOU ONLY SIGHED!*
*WITHHELD YOUR HAND, FROM PUNISHMENT*
*BORE A DEATH, THAT – FOR ME WAS MEANT!!*

*HOW MUCH ALIKE, A LITTLE MOSQUITO*

*MY CALLOUS LIFE, AND THOUGHTS DO FLOW!*
*WHILE I, IN CRUELTY, AM FULLY FILLED*
*HOPE IN MY HEART – YOU HAVE INSTILLED!!*
*THE VERY BLOOD, I BROUGHT TO STRIFE*
*HAS GIVEN ME, ETERNAL LIFE!*
*THE VERY LOVE, THAT CAME TO SAVE*
*HOW VERY FOOLISHLY, I, DID MISLAY!!*

19.04.2007

# We Worship You...

*We worship you!*
*We worship you!*
*O Lord God Our Father!*

*We bow our heads!*
*We bow our heads!*
*In presence great we gather!*

*We bend our knees!*
*We bend our knees!*
*As our tongues do confess!*

*We loudly proclaim!*
*We loudly proclaim!*
*The Saviour is Lord Jesus!*

*We lift our hearts!*
*We lift our hearts!!*
*To the only God in heaven!*

*We surrender now!*
*We surrender now!*
*Our hearts, Lord do amend!*

**24.4.2007**

# Immanuel

Immanuel,
Immanuel
God the Father, Immanuel
Immanuel,
Immanuel
Jesus Christ, Immanuel
Immanuel,
Immanuel
Holy Spirit, Immanuel
Immanuel,
Immanuel
God with us, Immanuel
Immanuel,
Immanuel
God within, Immanuel
Immanuel,
Immanuel
God Forever, Immanuel
Immanuel,
Immanuel
Holy Trinity, Immanuel

21.06.2007

# Senses........!

*O how blind, I am O' LORD,*
*despite the wonders that I see!*

*O how deaf, my ears do seem,*
*inspite of all, sweet sounds I hear!!*

*How much I sense, your daily touch,*
*still I reject, your tender feel!*

*Paths I tread, filled with sweet scent,*
*but to imbibe your grace, I fail!!*

*O Lord your goodness, is everywhere,*
*however your love to taste, still unaware!*

*O Lord I pray, in my conscience fill,*
*Love, Care and grateful thoughts,*

*Quickened and conscious may it be,*
*your loving mercy to embrace!!*

25.06.2007

# Holy Spirit

It is the Holy Spirit
That enables me each day
To do the things I am to do,
To speak good words, and pray!

It is the Holy Spirit
That mends my aching heart
To show some love to anyone
Who feels life's coming apart!

It is the Holy Spirit
That strengthens my weak flesh
So that, I could - in my turn
A struggling neighbour refresh!

It is the Holy Spirit
That guides my wandering mind,
Towards My awesome Father,
Who is love, patient and kind!

It is the Holy Spirit,
That puts praise into my soul
To give me hope - deep within,
And blesses with treasures untold!

It is the Holy Spirit,
That saves my heart from sin,
No matter when I would depart
He'd open the doors to Heaven!

**21.4.2007**

# Swine Flu

*Just a cough or a sneeze,*
*Or a shrill breathless wheeze,*
*Frowning people turn around,*
*Poor nose you quickly squeeze,*
*Hoping loud it's not the swine,*
*As you stifle a long whine,*
*Whilst the "Doc" looks at you,*
*As would a specimen from the zoo!*

*Pictures galore, do nothing great,*
*Only your fear, increasingly spate,*
*For t'was just yesterday,*
*When the dreaded seemed at bay,*
*Yet today a tiny one's, future bright,*
*Lies cold, shattered - an unbearable sight!*

*Sending up a prayer,*
*Distraught in despair,*
*Painfully you realize-*
*That......*
*there's nothing to save you,*
*But God's grace that's true.*

12.08.2009

# What am I?

As tiny a creature as I am,
I wonder how you, Lord
Care to look for me!

So much do you love me, Lord,
I'm ashamed my sinful heart
To bare in front of you!

I'm not even a bit worthy of
great mercy You bestowed
Through your Only Son!

Of what am I that you care,
To sacrifice your Dear One
For someone wretched as me!

Am hardly a speck in this
Mighty Universe of yours,
Where even stars twinkle praise!

Though this greedy soul of mine
Swallow your kindness whole
Causes pain through sinful deeds!

Oh what lowly depths I go
You, Still lift me up each time
With only thanks to You Lord!

You save this hopeless soul of mine,
What am I?

# X'mas

Too many people celebrate 'loud -
The rollicking madness spreading out,
like a fire burning up its shroud,
Merrily dancing without a care.

Not even knowing the reason,
for having joined in the fair.
Expressing joy in a stupor,
Beyond the occasion's share.

Solemn instead it should have been
with family and friends in
the confines of a home,
Lilting soft music and a little red wine.

To celebrate the birth of the
Eternal life giver,
No longer does it stay
what it was meant to be.

Don't overkill comrades,
is it too hard to realise
what joy can overtake,
Even wrath can surpass!

Over all the hours spent in
joyful merry making,
Spend a true moment for goodness
and the sake of the Saviour's mercy!

# Destiny

Don't spend your treasures
To save my life
Let me go
The natural way.

What God has ordained
Don't try to change
As whatever destined
Will come what may.

My life no more shows
Any promise at all
And it's purpose
Appears lost
Somewhere along the way.

So selfish it seems
If I waste your time
Or ask you to spend
All of your precious dimes
On saving this unworthy
Life of mine
That's destined to be
Just a mime!

It is not meet
For me to entreat
Another lease of life
When what was given
To me at birth
I've squandered
Thus far, to waste.

# Pains and Needles!

Just a faint blur was all that I saw
Wonderin' from where the pain so raw
Traveled past my swollen head
As what'd happened I'd always dread

T'was in fact not my misdeed
That now I face the haloed breed
Armed with thistle, thorns and pricks
They jab away trashing all my tricks

My swollen eyes not able to behold
Beautiful angels bringing pain untold
Armed with needles they do profess
To undo pain, more pain they ingress

I would not be cribbing all the while
But it's because of a speeding imbecile
Now I am bandaged and scrutinized
As he scooted off, I lay half paralyzed

Adding misery is a stream of friends
Promptly quizzing me in latest trends
Even as I lay in shock of this anecdote
One chap coolly my broken arm smote

As I almost fell off shrieking in pain
Said something careless in words plain
Yet more well meaning comrades of mine
Heap varieties of unwanted things in line

Thanks for those hours visitors are barred
Or for life I am sure to have been scarred
One way or other trouble seems to follow
Knowing well t'is pain that I can't swallow

01.01.2011

# The Broken Church!

the coffers are empty
the coffins are full
the graveyards are
calling me, kith and kin

spirits of love have
slipped far below
the purpose of living
a lingering shadow

the calling and prayers
rebound off our walls
the worshippers wailing
are painful to the ears

the show goes on
as it hitherto did
but the One no more stands
where once Holiness stood

tearful spirits in turmoil
gleefully hide remorse
for where once was a temple
stands now a broken church!
Only a Holy spirit
pervading through broken hearts
can provide the calm we seek
provided we become meek!

true love like He had

for sinners like us
is only the breakthrough
out of this unholy mess

two vines in one spot
soon die in quick time
let oneness be seen
be heard and in us shine

how much longer
these jabs and jibes
time to move forward
and bring back good vibes

should we repeat
what they did to our Lord
t'is passed time to mend
the Church - and...so too
our hardened hearts!

# I Wanna be There

I WANNA BE THERE WHEN IT HAPPENS
TO GREET HIM WHEN HE COMES
I WANNA BE DRESSED IN WHITEST WHITE
AND ANSWER THOSE TRUMPET CALLS!!

I WANNA SHOUT HIS NAME ALOUD
AND LIFT IT UP ON HIGH
I WANNA SAY IT 'HEAD OF TIME
SO THAT I WON'T BE LEFT BEHIND!!

I WANNA SEE HIS GLORIOUS FACE
AND FEEL HIS MIGHTY TOUCH
I WANNA BE TRULY BORN AGAIN
AND FROM ALL SIN FORGIV'N!!

I WANNA MEET HIM ON HIS WAY
WHEN HE COMES TO TAKE US BACK
I WANNA SEE THOSE AWESOME SIGHTS
WHEN HE COMES ON JUDGMENT DAY!!

I WANNA BE THERE WHEN IT HAPPENS
WITNESS THAT GOLDEN REIGN
I WANNA BE RIGHT NEXT TO HIM
AND A PLACE IN HEAVEN TO GAIN!!

06.03.05

# Finally

Get ready for the funeral rain,
there's not much time left now,
It's going to become dark again
Time to take the ultimate bow!

A little squeeze both left and right
As what's mortal finally lies still,
Filled in with tears and roses tight
Across the room, sadness to fill!

Into a journey to eternal bliss
With no sense of time or mile,
Many a relative entwine and kiss
Albeit with a grievous smile!

Mighty a lid, engraved slams shut,
on all Earthly deeds, words and acts
Into the ground, away from the rut
Am lowered if done with the pacts!

People throw in a handful of rubble
While my struggles seem to end
The golden nail an end trouble
'Cause my tongue no more can offend!

An anniversary later a tomb appears
to mark my absence on this Earth
For many, time has dried up the tears,
With hope I'm midst Heaven's mirth!

**27.04.2015**